The Orphan & the Giant

The Nunavummi reading series is a Nunavut-developed levelled book series that supports literacy development while teaching readers about the people, traditions, and environment of the Canadian Arctic.

Nunavummi

Published in Canada by Nunavummi, an imprint of Inhabit Education Books Inc. | www.inhabiteducation.com

Inhabit Education Books Inc.
(Iqaluit) P.O. Box 2129, Iqaluit, Nunavut, X0A 1H0
(Toronto) 191 Eglinton Avenue East, Suite 301, Toronto, Ontario, M4P 1K1

Printed in Canada.

Library and Archives Canada Cataloguing in Publication

Title: The orphan & the giant / written by Neil Christopher ; illustrated by Jim Nelson.
Other titles: Orphan and the giant
Names: Christopher, Neil, 1972- author. | Nelson, Jim, 1962- illustrator.
Description: Series statement: Nunavummi reading series
Identifiers: Canadiana 2020020727X | ISBN 9781774500705 (hardcover)
Classification: LCC PS8605.H754 O77 2020 | DDC jC813/.6—dc23

ISBN: 978-1-77450-070-5

INHABIT
EDUCATION
BOOKS

The Orphan & the Giant

WRITTEN BY

Neil Christopher

ILLUSTRATED BY

Jim Nelson

Long ago, there was an orphan who was looking for a place to call home. This little orphan was clever and resourceful. Even though he was young, he was attentive and observant, and he had learned many things from the Elders he had met.

On this particular day, the orphan was enjoying the fish he had recently caught. He was sharing some of the fish with a seagull that had been following him. Since he was alone in the world, he decided it was nice to have company, even if it was a seagull.

"Here is some fish," the orphan said. "I guess you are alone, too. You are welcome to join me on my search for a home if you would like."

"Squawk," the seagull replied, as if to say, "Yes, I would like to join you."

4

"Everyone needs a home!"
the orphan said to the bird.
"I will find a home for us."

As they ate their fish, the
orphan thought about his
recent adventures. He
had outsmarted the huge
*amautalik** that wandered the
land. He had also tricked the
*qallupilluit*** that lived under
the sea ice.

*amautalik (a-MOW-ta-lik):
mythological ogress that steals
children on the land
**qallupilluit (QAL-lu-PIL-lu-it):
mythological sea creatures that
steal children through ice cracks

6

"I need to be careful," the orphan said to himself. "It is dangerous travelling alone."

"Squawk, squawk," yelled the seagull, not wanting to be forgotten.

"Sorry, seagull!" said the orphan. "You are right. I am not alone."

After some rest, the orphan and the seagull
continued on their way. The orphan wasn't hungry
anymore, and he was happy to be walking again.

The sun was out, and there were
very few clouds in the sky.
The wind was blowing a bit,
so there were not even
any mosquitoes.

It was a perfect day
for walking.

The orphan came upon a small herd of caribou. He watched them as they moved slowly over the ground. The orphan tried to imagine how he could catch a caribou with what he had in his bag. He was thinking hard about this idea and did not hear the seagull calling him.

"Squawk…squawk…squaaaawk!"

"**What are you upset about?**" the orphan asked the seagull.

Suddenly, the sky grew dark. This was strange, as the orphan couldn't see any clouds in the sky.

The little orphan turned to see what was causing such a large shadow.

There stood a giant!

The little orphan could not believe how large this being was.

The seagull flew away in fear. Before the orphan could run or even think about what to do, the giant reached down and picked him up.

"You are a strange little thing," said the giant. "Are you a lemming?"

"N...n...no!" said the orphan bravely. "I...I am a boy!"

"Hmmmm, a boy? Well, I guess that could be true, as I have never seen a lemming that can talk," said the giant, puzzled.

"**What are you doing all alone?**" the giant asked the orphan.

"**I am looking for a home**," explained the orphan. "**You see, I am an orphan. I don't have a family. I have been looking for a place to live where I belong.**"

The giant wrinkled his forehead and thought silently for a few moments before asking his next question.

"**Would you like to join me on my trip? I am walking to the salt sea to fish for sculpin. We would have a great adventure and hopefully a feast after I catch a sculpin.**"

The little orphan couldn't imagine how sculpin could be a feast for the giant, but he liked the sound of the adventure, and the giant seemed nice.

"Yes, I would like to join you on your fishing trip," said the orphan.

The giant was pleased. **"People call me *Inukpak*,"*** he explained to the orphan. **"I am pleased to have company on my walk."**

*Inukpak (e-NOOK-pak): giant

Inukpak put the orphan on his shoulder and began to walk across the land.

"Hold on tight!" Inukpak suggested before he started walking.

The orphan had never been so high up. He could see very far in all directions.

Inukpak's long strides allowed them to move very quickly over the land.

As they were walking, they passed a large herd of caribou. The orphan was so excited that he yelled into the giant's ear, **"Look at all the caribou! If we catch one, we could have a feast!"**

"Those are not caribou!" Inukpak said, giggling. "They are much too small. They must be lemmings or *siksiit*,* or something like that. You cannot have a feast with animals that are so small."

The orphan did not know what to say. So he just shrugged and said, "Okay."

*siksiit (sik-SEET): plural of siksik, or ground squirrel

In a short time, the two travellers crossed a great distance. Inukpak easily stepped across rivers, climbed up mountains, and waded through huge lakes.

Eventually, they reached the sea.

"We are here!" Inukpak announced. **"Travelling always gives me an appetite. You stay here where it is safe. I will find us a delicious fish!"**

Inukpak placed the little orphan on a hill, and then he walked into the sea.

Although Inukpak waded far into the water, it didn't rise much higher than his thighs. That is how large Inukpak was!

The orphan watched as Inukpak became very still and stared into the water. The giant didn't move for hours. By the time Inukpak had found what he was looking for, the sun had moved across the sky.

Inukpak suddenly plunged his hands into the seawater.

The giant struggled and struggled, and then he pulled out a huge bowhead. It was the largest animal the little orphan had ever seen!

Inukpak carried it back to the shore. His quick steps caused a huge wave.

"**Oh, no! Inukpak, slow down!**" the orphan yelled. But Inukpak did not hear him, and he continued to rush toward shore with his huge catch.

The orphan ran farther up the hill to avoid the seawater, and he climbed to the top of a large boulder.

Seawater filled the beach and almost reached where the orphan had climbed.

When the water moved back toward the sea, there were fish flapping everywhere on the shore.

"You see, little one? I have brought us a feast!" Inukpak announced.

"Yes…yes, you have!" the orphan replied, looking at all the fish on the beach.

The two friends spent the next few days eating, drying meat, and sharing stories.

Finally, it was time to move on. The orphan and Inukpak had filled their packs with enough food for many days of travel.

"I am heading west to where it is hilly. Would you like to come?" asked the great giant.

The orphan thought for a few minutes before answering.

"I have enjoyed travelling and fishing with you. And you have been very kind and generous to me. But I am looking for a place to call home, and I don't think I will find it in the west."

Inukpak looked carefully at the orphan and sighed. **"I understand,"** he finally said. **"I hope you find your home."**

And with that, Inukpak stood up, wiped his eyes, and stretched. He turned to start on his journey. But before he left, Inukpak crouched back down and faced the little orphan.

"If you ever need help, just let me know. I always help my friends."

"That is very kind of you, but how could I get a message to you?" the orphan asked.

"Just call my name. I have really big ears!" Inukpak said with a big smile on his face.

And with that, Inukpak began his walk. Within a few strides he was far away on the horizon. Once again, the orphan was alone on his journey.

Almost as soon as Inukpak was gone, the seagull flew down and landed on a nearby rock.

"Well, hello, seagull. Where have you been?"

"Squawk, squawk!" answered the seagull.

"Have you been waiting for the giant to leave?" the orphan said with a giggle. "Well, let's see what we find over those hills."

The little orphan now found himself far away from where he started. He was excited to explore this new place.

The orphan and the seagull headed out to see what adventures the new days would bring.

Inuktitut Glossary

Notes on Inuktitut pronunciation: There are some sounds in Inuktitut that may be unfamiliar to English speakers. The pronunciations below convey those sounds in the following ways:

- A double vowel (for example, *aa*, *ee*) creates a long vowel sound.
- Capitalized letters indicate the emphasis.
- **q** is a "uvular" sound, which is a sound that comes from the very back of the throat (the uvula). This is different from the **k** sound, which is the same as the typical English **k** sound.
- **ll** is a rolled "l" sound.

For more Inuktitut and Inuinnaqtun pronunciation resources, please visit inhabiteducation.com/inuithipingit.

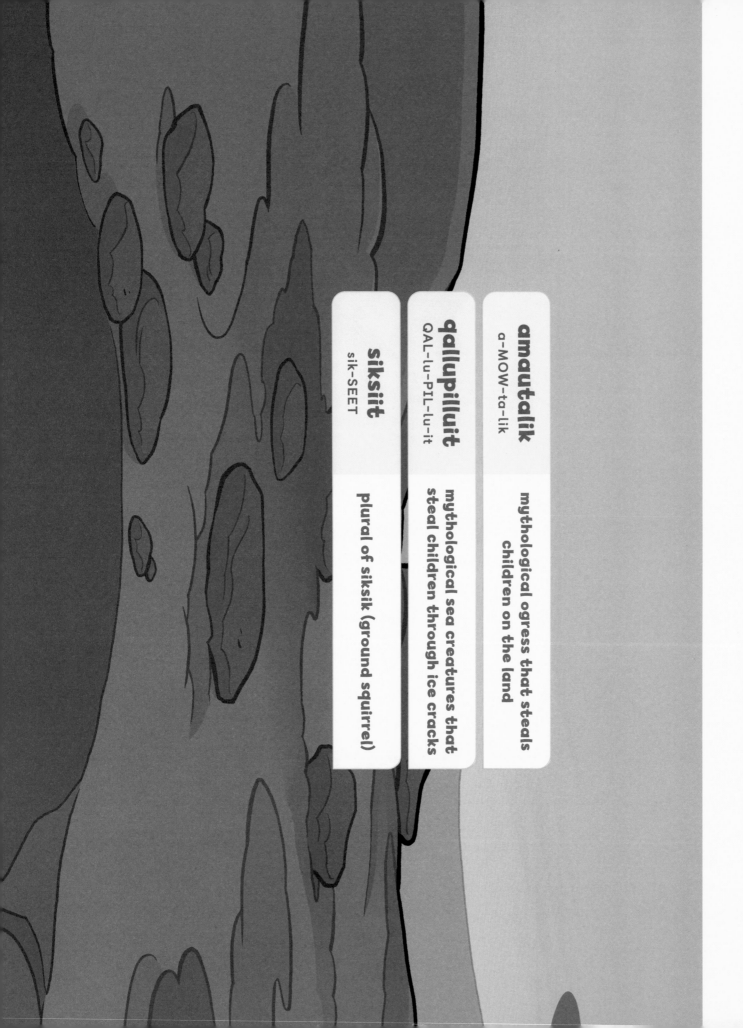

| **amautalik** a-MOW-ta-lik | mythological ogress that steals children on the land |

| **qallupilluit** QAL-lu-PIL-lu-it | mythological sea creatures that steal children through ice cracks |

| **siksiit** sik-SEET | plural of siksik (ground squirrel) |

Nunavummi
Reading Series

The Nunavummi reading series is a Nunavut-developed levelled book series that supports literacy development while teaching readers about the people, traditions, and environment of the Canadian Arctic.

Level 11
- 24–32 pages
- Sentences become complex and varied
- Varied punctuation
- Dialogue is included in fiction texts and is necessary to understand the story
- Readers rely more on the words than the images to decode the text

12
- 24–40 pages
- Sentences are complex and vary in length
- Lots of varied punctuation
- Dialogue is included in fiction texts and is necessary to understand the story
- Readers rely on the words to decode the text; images are present but only somewhat supportive

Level 13
- 24–56 pages
- Sentences can be more complicated and are not always restricted to a structure that readers are familiar with
- Some unfamiliar themes and genres are introduced
- Readers rely on the words to decode the text; images are present but only somewhat supportive

Fountas & Pinnell Text Level: P

This book has been officially levelled using the F&P Text Level Gradient™ Leveling System.